HiT entertainment

First published in Great Britain 2011 by Dean
an imprint of Egmont UK Limited
239 Kensington High Street,
London W8 6SA

All rights reserved
ISBN 978 0 6035 6604 2
1 3 5 7 9 10 8 6 4 2
Printed in Malaysia

Fireman Sam™

Dinosaur Hunt

It was a sunny day in Pontypandy. Norman was looking for treasure.

He searched all over the beach but could only find bits of driftwood.

"Hello, Norman," said Trevor. "Looking for treasure, I see?"

"Yeah!" Norman sighed. "But there's no treasure anywhere!"

Suddenly, Trevor saw something. "Norman, it's a fossil!" cried Trevor. "Long ago, there were dinosaurs in Pontypandy," Trevor explained. "You can see their footsteps preserved in stone, like this . . ."

"WOW!" cried Norman. "I'm going to hunt for real dinosaur footprints!"

"Not now, Norman," Trevor warned. "The tide is coming in and you could get stranded!"

He gave Norman the fossil and they headed into the village.

At the quay, Norman spotted the twins and rushed over to show them the fossil Trevor had found.

"James! Sarah!" cried Norman. "I bet you've never seen a baby dinosaur before."

Norman pulled the fossil out of his pocket.

"That's not a dinosaur!" laughed James. "It's a fossil. Dinosaurs are extinct."

"No they're not!" Norman said. "I saw one on the beach."

The twins exchanged a glance. "Did not!" cried Sarah.

Norman walked off, sniggering. "I'll show them," he muttered.

A little later on, Norman was in the backyard of the supermarket.

He was hammering something together out of driftwood.

Finally, his creation was complete. Norman held up a huge wooden foot on the end of a long stick. It looked just like a dinosaur footprint!

Norman went back to the beach and found a spot close to the shore. He stood on the wooden foot, held onto the stick, then hopped three times across the sand.

Norman had made a trail of **HUGE DINOSAUR FOOTPRINTS!**

"I bet the twins will think they are real!" Norman smiled.

Norman picked up the dinosaur leg and went to find the twins.

At the quay, he heard a loud noise. Norman threw the dinosaur foot behind him and hurried off.

James and Sarah were outside the Wholefish Café.

"Want to come on a dinosaur hunt?" Norman asked the twins.

"Don't be daft!" giggled Sarah.

"Maybe you're just too scared?" Norman shrugged. Then he walked off towards the beach.

The twins didn't want to look afraid, so they followed after Norman.

Trevor was driving his bus along the quay. He noticed Norman and the twins heading off to the coast.

Suddenly, he had to brake sharply. Something was blocking the road!

"What in the world!" Trevor cried. He was just about to drive over Norman's wooden dinosaur foot!

Meanwhile, Norman was leading the twins along the beach.

"Be on the lookout, you two!" Norman instructed his friends.

Suddenly, James spotted something in the distance. He ran up to the tracks Norman had made earlier.

"OOOH!" cried James, pointing at the marks in the sand. "Look, Sarah, there are dinosaur footprints!"

"I told you I saw a dinosaur!" Norman said. "Come on, I'm going to catch it!" He quickly ran off into the distance.

James and Sarah followed after Norman but they couldn't find him anywhere.

"Norman! Norman!" called James.

Suddenly, a strange sound came out of the cave in a nearby cliff . . .

"GRRRR! GRRRR!"

"It's the dinosaur!" cried James, and he hurried into the cave.

Sarah sighed. That was no dinosaur, just silly Norman playing tricks again.

She glanced back along the beach. The sea was a lot closer than before. The tide was coming in!

Sarah ran towards the cave that her brother had just entered.

"James!" Sarah shouted.
"We have to get back!"

James crept into the cave, following the strange growls.

Suddenly, something moved. James tiptoed closer. But instead of a dinosaur, he found Norman!

"Oh!" realised James. "It was you!"

"No!" lied Norman. "It was the dinosaur!" He pointed deeper into the cave.

"Are you sure?" James hesitated.

"Go and see for yourself if you don't believe me!" cried Norman.

"OK, I will," replied James.

As they went further into the cave, neither heard Sarah's warning.

Outside, the water was getting closer and closer to the mouth of the cave.

Sarah tried calling to James and Norman again, but there was no reply.

She decided to get help and ran back along the shore as quickly as she could.

Back in the cave, Norman and James had not found any dinosaurs.

"I knew there was never a dinosaur!" said James, as they walked back towards the entrance of the cave.

Suddenly, they both screamed. The mouth of the cave was flooded!

"We're trapped!" cried Norman.

Outside the Wholefish Café, Bronwyn was very worried.

"Everything OK?" asked Trevor.

"I can't find the twins!" Bronwyn said. "Have you seen them?"

"I think I saw them heading to the beach," remembered Trevor.

"The tide's in," realised Bronwyn. "I'm going to call Fireman Sam!"

Minutes later, the Fire Station alarm bell rang. **Action Stations!**

"Norman and the twins are missing!" Station Officer Steele called. "Last seen on the beach."

Penny and Sam headed to the beach in Venus.

Once there, they launched the lifeboat, Neptune, and sped into the sea with a splash.

Meanwhile, Tom took off in his helicopter. He flew along the cliffs, searching for the children.

Suddenly he spotted Sarah.

"Come in, Sam," Tom called on the radio. "Sarah is about five hundred metres along the North Bay Cliffs."

"Thanks, Tom," Sam answered. "We see her too."

Penny steered Neptune towards Sarah, who was stranded on a rock. The lifeboat pulled up alongside her.

"I've got you," said Sam, lifting Sarah on board. "But where are Norman and James?"

Back in the cave, Norman and James were very frightened.

"HEEEEELP!" they cried.

Suddenly, Norman saw something.

"Look, James!" screamed Norman. "It's a sea monster!"

James followed Norman's gaze. Something emerged from the water . . . it was Penny in her diving suit!

"Hello, boys," Penny said, climbing out. Norman felt very silly.

"Don't be scared," reassured Penny. "I'll get you both out."

Shortly after, the children were safely in the Wholefish Café. Norman knew he was in trouble.

"You should know that the changing tide is dangerous!" Sam reminded the children.

"But Norman said he saw a dinosaur!" James cried.

"Well it must have been a very old dinosaur," chuckled Trevor. "I think I've found his walking stick!"

Trevor pulled out Norman's wooden dinosaur leg and hobbled around the room.

Everyone laughed, even silly Norman!

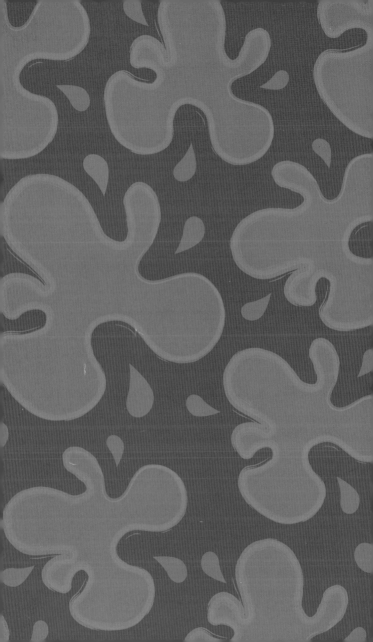